First published 2012 by Walker Books Ltd
87 Vauxhall Walk, London SE11 5HJ

2 4 6 8 10 9 7 5 3 1

Text © 2012 Sam McBratney
Illustrations © 2012 Anita Jeram

Illustrated in the style of Anita Jeram by Andy Wagner and Debbie Tarbett

Guess How Much I Love You™ is a registered
trademark of Walker Books Ltd, London

The right of Sam McBratney to be identified as author of this
work has been asserted by him in accordance with
the Copyright, Designs and Patents Act 1988

This book has been typeset in Cochin

Printed in China

British Library Cataloguing in
Publication Data: a catalogue record
for this book is available from the
British Library

ISBN 978-1-4063-2310-8 (hbk)
ISBN 978-1-4063-4482-0 (pbk)

www.walker.co.uk

Guess How Much I Love You
HERE, THERE AND EVERYWHERE

Sam McBratney

WALKER BOOKS
AND SUBSIDIARIES
LONDON • BOSTON • SYDNEY • AUCKLAND

The Hiding Tree

Little Nutbrown Hare woke up one
morning and could hardly believe his eyes.
His favourite tree, the Hiding Tree,
was lying on the ground.

He called it the Hiding Tree
because it was hollow inside and
you could easily hide in there.
Not any more, though. There had
been a storm in the night.

Big Nutbrown Hare scrambled up through
the roots and stood on the trunk of the tree.

That is a long way up, thought
Little Nutbrown Hare.

With a hop and a skip, Big Nutbrown Hare
went to the other end and peeped
through the leaves.

"Are you coming?"

"No, it's too high,"
said Little Nutbrown Hare
– and off he went to look
for interesting things
on the ground.

In the afternoon he played hide-and-seek with
Big Nutbrown Hare; and when it was his turn to
hide, he came once more to where his favourite tree,
the Hiding Tree, was lying on its side.

That would be the best hiding-place ever!

Up through the roots he scrambled. I could
go over and hide in the leaves, he thought.

And right now Big Nutbrown Hare
was counting! In a moment
he would sing out,
"Here I come,
ready or not!"

With some careful hops … then a bit of a wobble …
and one last good jump …

Little Nutbrown Hare went along
the trunk of the tree to hide among
the branches and the leaves.

Now it was important to be absolutely still.

Big Nutbrown Hare looked here,

and there …

and everywhere

– or so he thought.

"I give up,"
he shouted at last.
"You must have the best
hiding-place ever!"

Little Nutbrown Hare
came tumbling down from
the Hiding Tree.

Big Nutbrown Hare was amazed.

"But I thought you were afraid to go up there!"

"I'm not afraid any more,"
laughed Little Nutbrown Hare.

On Cloudy Mountain

Little Nutbrown Hare and
Big Nutbrown Hare set out one morning
to climb the Cloudy Mountain. They liked to
be up high and look down at the fields; and
besides, some of the plants that grew on
Cloudy Mountain were very tasty.

After lunch, Little Nutbrown Hare
played in the waterfalls among the rocks.
And then – better still – he found some
dandelions just ready for blowing.

One … two … three … *whooo*.

Half of a seedhead was gone.

"That's good blowing,"
said Big Nutbrown Hare.

One ... two ... three ... *whooo*.

Little Nutbrown Hare did an even better blow.

Away went the dandelion seeds,

almost every one.

And there were so many more,

all ready to be blown!

Big Nutbrown Hare had noticed something,
however. The clouds were coming further
and further down the mountain.
Soon they wouldn't be able to see a thing.

"We have to go home now," he said.

"I'm still blowing!" said Little Nutbrown Hare.

"I know," said Big Nutbrown Hare,
"but the clouds are coming
   and we have to go."

You're spoiling all my fun,
Little Nutbrown Hare
was thinking.

But the mist was
getting thicker
every moment.

Which way was up

and which was down?

All of a sudden Big Nutbrown Hare
was right there beside him.

"Come with me now," he said.

Together they ran
down the mountain,
out of the clouds, and
into the sunny day below.

"Well, that certainly was an adventure!"
said Big Nutbrown Hare. "I'm sorry
I had to stop your fun like that."

"You nearly got lost!"
said Little Nutbrown Hare.

"Nearly," smiled Big Nutbrown Hare,
glancing up once more at
Cloudy Mountain.
"But what matters is
– I found you."

The Far Field

Early one morning Little Nutbrown Hare
ran all the way to the Far Field.
He called it the Far Field because it was further
than the Hiding Tree ... over the river ...
and beyond the Cloudy Mountain.

He discovered an interesting hole beneath
the trees, and wondered what was in there.

"Come away," said a voice. "It's best
not to bother with holes in the ground."

It was Big Nutbrown Hare watching over him.

So Little Nutbrown Hare came away
from the hole and jumped over
some toadstools instead.

There was a pond nearby. The leaves of the water-plants looked like stepping stones across the water.

"No, no," said a voice,
"that water might be deep. Come away."

It was Big Nutbrown Hare
telling him to be careful.

So Little Nutbrown Hare skipped away from
the pond and found another place to play.

Then, in the thickness of the meadow grass, he discovered a birds' nest. Four speckled eggs lay there, lovely and smooth.

"Come away," someone whispered.
"Birds don't like anyone near their nest."
Once again Big Nutbrown Hare was close by.

Together they hopped away from the nest with its
precious eggs, to search the meadow grass
for juicy plants to eat.

Later that day, Little Nutbrown Hare went
back to the interesting hole beneath the trees.
Still he couldn't see a thing in there,
which made him wonder all the more.

What would be down a hole like that?

He looked around and saw no one else.
He was quite alone.

I think I might go down there,
thought Little Nutbrown Hare…

Then a voice said, "No.
Dark holes are dangerous."

This time it was his own little voice
inside his head, and it was
telling him to be careful.

So Little Nutbrown Hare came away from
the hole and chased some daddy-long-legs
through the Far Field instead.

Coming Home

Little Nutbrown Hare and Big Nutbrown Hare were westering home at the end of the day.

"Can you guess the place I like best in the whole world?" said Little Nutbrown Hare, who loved to play games.

"Your favourite place?" asked Big Nutbrown Hare.

"Yes. In the world."

Big Nutbrown Hare began to think.
He knew that Little Nutbrown Hare
liked lots of places, but which one
did he like best?

"Is it … Cloudy Mountain?"

"No, that's too high up."

On they went, hopping home together.
Big Nutbrown Hare was thinking so hard
that he didn't watch where he was going.

"Wet feet!" he said. "Ah –
is your favourite place …
the river?"

"No," laughed Little Nutbrown Hare.
"That's too wet."

On they went hopping home, until
Big Nutbrown Hare suddenly stopped.
He'd just had a good idea.

"Is your favourite place *across* the river?
 Could it be … the Far Field?"

"No, that's too far away."

On they ran quite quickly now, for the sun
was sinking fast. Then Big Nutbrown Hare
spotted something that made him think.

"Do we play games in this place
you're thinking of ? Could it be
… the Hiding Tree?"

"No. But my favourite place has some leaves."

Goodness me! thought Big Nutbrown Hare.
Not Cloudy Mountain. Not the river.
Not the Far Field. Some leaves,
but not the Hiding Tree.

"Well … I think you'll
have to tell me,"
he said at last.

"We're here! *Home* is my best place of all."

"Well, of course!"
said Big Nutbrown Hare.
"I should have guessed!"

The early stars were shining already.

Big Nutbrown Hare settled
Little Nutbrown Hare into his bed of leaves,
where soon he closed his eyes.

"And where *you* are," whispered
Big Nutbrown Hare, "is the best place
in the whole world for me."